BOOMING BELLA

Carol Ann Williams

ILLUSTRATED BY
Tatjana Mai-Wyss

G. P. Putnam's Sons

For Matthew.—C.A.W.

For Louisa and Nora.—T.M.

G. P. PUTNAM'S SONS

A division of Penguin Young Readers Group. Published by The Penguin Group.

Penguin Group (USA) Inc., 375 Hudson Street, New York, NY 10014, U.S.A.

Penguin Group (Canada), 90 Eglinton Avenue East, Suite 700, Toronto, Ontario M4P 2Y3, Canada

(a division of Pearson Penguin Canada Inc.).

Penguin Books Ltd, 80 Strand, London WC2R 0RL, England.

Penguin Ireland, 25 St. Stephen's Green, Dublin 2, Ireland (a division of Penguin Books Ltd.).

Penguin Group (Australia), 250 Camberwell Road, Camberwell, Victoria 3124, Australia

(a division of Pearson Australia Group Pty Ltd).

Penguin Books India Pvt Ltd, 11 Community Centre, Panchsheel Park, New Delhi - 110 017, India.

Penguin Group (NZ), 67 Apollo Drive, Rosedale, North Shore 0632, New Zealand

(a division of Pearson NZ Ltd).

Penguin Books (South Africa) (Pty) Ltd, 24 Sturdee Avenue, Rosebank, Johannesburg 2196, South Africa.

Penguin Books Ltd, Registered Offices: 80 Strand, London WC2R 0RL, England.

Published simultaneously in Canada. Manufactured in China by South China Printing Co. Ltd.

Design by Marikka Tamura. Text set in Administer.

The art was done with watercolor, gouache and collage on watercolor paper.

Library of Congress Cataloging-in-Publication Data

Williams, Carol Ann. Booming Bella / Carol Ann Williams ; illustrated by Tatjana Mai-Wyss.

p. cm. Summary: Bella's enthusiasm, and her very loud voice, almost ruin a field trip to the art museum,

but when she accidentally gets on the wrong bus at the end of the day, her shouting comes in handy.

[1. Voice—Fiction. 2. Noise—Fiction. 3. Behavior—Fiction. 4. School field trips—Fiction.]

I. Mai-Wyss, Tatjana, 1972– ill. II. Title. PZ7.W655874Bo 2008 [E]—dc22 2006008245

ISBN 978-0-399-24277-9

10 9 8 7 6 5 4 3 2 1

Bella flung open the door of her classroom and boomed, "HEY, EVERYBODY! Today's the class trip! I've got my water bottle! And a CAMERA my dad gave me!

I CAN TAKE PICTURES OF US ALL!"

"It's time to go," said the teacher.
"HOORAY!" shouted Bella. "WE'RE ON OUR WAY!"

She darted ahead. The teacher quickly grabbed her hand.

Outside, when the big yellow bus with the purple giraffe in the window opened its door, Bella hopped in and hollered to the driver, "WE'RE GOING TO THE ART MUSEUM!"

The driver blinked at her loud voice and said, "You don't need to yell."

"ISN'T THIS FUN!?" she exclaimed to the boy she plopped next to.

He covered his ears with his hands.

All along the way, Bella bounced and shouted at each familiar place they passed: "OH, THE LIBRARY! I LOVE THAT LIBRARY! EVERYBODY, LOOK! IT'S OUR VIDEO STORE! THERE'S MY FRIEND JENNIFER'S HOUSE!"

"You're giving me a headache," complained the girl in front of her.

A teacher came down the aisle and whispered to Bella, "Please use your inside voice."

"Okay," Bella whispered back.

But as the museum came into view, she screamed,
"THE MUSEUM! SEE IT!?

THERE IT IS!"

Bella's teacher took her hand to lead her out onto the sidewalk. She told her, "The museum is a quiet place. Remember, no hollering allowed."

"Okay," Bella whispered. "I'll remember."

She even tiptoed up the big front steps.

But inside the museum she hollered, "WOW! THIS PLACE IS BIG! IT'S HUGE!"

A nearby guard scowled and said, "Watch your manners, young lady."

"Sorry," Bella mouthed.

Then the museum guide led the class around. Her questions were so much fun, Bella shouted the answer to every one:

The guide stopped. "If you keep this up, I will not be able to continue." The woman stood in silence.

The whole class turned to look at Bella.

"You're ruining everything," a boy said.

Bella's face got red. She didn't mean to be loud—she just got so excited.

For the rest of the tour,
she didn't even look at
the beautiful paintings.
Bella wanted to go home.

When it was time, she ran as fast as she could for the bus. She jumped on just as the doors were closing.

"Take your seat," ordered the driver.

Bella looked at him. This was not the driver who had brought them. She hurried down the aisle. The children began to sing a song she'd never heard before.

She climbed onto a seat next to a strange big girl and poked her head out into the aisle. Where were her teachers? Where were the helping parents? She stood on the seat. Where was the purple giraffe in the window?

As the bus started to pull away from the curb, Bella realized she had gotten on the wrong bus.

She knew she was not supposed to holler.
It always got her in trouble. But this was an
emergency. In the loudest voice she'd ever used,
she bellowed, "STOP THE BUS!
I'M ON THE WRONG BUS!"

All the children stopped singing.
"Who are you?" cried a teacher.
"I'm Bella and I'm on the wrong bus!"

"Stop the bus!" the teacher shouted. The bus
bumped to a halt.

From outside they could now hear Bella's teacher yelling,
"STOP! STOP! YOU HAVE THE WRONG STUDENT!"

The driver opened the door to let Bella out.

Her teacher rushed to her. "Oh, Bella, you scared us."
"Good thing she has a loud voice," said the other teacher.

"Yes," her teacher said, "sometimes it's a very good thing."
Bella sighed.

Then she saw her classmates smiling and waving from the windows of her own bus. She raced toward them, held out her camera, and hollered, "HEY, EVERYBODY! SAY CHEESE!"

And they all hollered back, "CHEESE!"
This was the best trip Bella had ever been on.